The Wild Horses
of
Summer Bay

*To Connor & Lauren,
I hope you enjoy
the story!
Margarida Kondak*

By Margarida Kondak
Illustrated by Mary Kondak

ISBN: 1-890692-06-9

Printed in Korea

Wizard Works
P.O. Box 1125
Homer, Alaska 99603
907-235-8757; wizard@xyz.net
www.xyz.net/~wizard

We lovingly dedicate this book to Patrick Michael Kondak

On the windswept island of Unalaska there lived a wild horse. He wandered alone in the hills and valleys that surround Summer Bay with only the eagles and ravens as sometime companions. The native plants and grasses nourished him and he had the coldest, cleanest mountain streams to quench his thirst.

His hide was dark, darker than brown, but not quite black. Belonging to no one, he had no name but was known in the village as "the dark horse." He was heavy, stout and slightly sway-backed. Unlike a common barnyard horse, his coat was not smooth and shiny, but rough and dulled by the wind and salt spray. A matted mane lay on his neck and his watery brown eyes were partially hidden by a shaggy forelock. He had large yellow teeth and un-shod, untrimmed hooves.

Although he was not very tolerant of people, the children of the village knew that the dark horse loved carrots and apples and such, and many went to Summer Bay with a bag of bruised fruit, hoping for a chance to offer him a treat.

One child was especially patient, and never gave up his dream of getting close to the dark horse.

The thin, black-haired boy stood on a small rise and searched the line of hills leading away from the rocky beach. His excitement grew as he spotted the dark figure against the golden tufts of grass. Clutching tightly to the wilted carrots in his hand, he moved slowly toward the wild horse.

The dark horse lifted his head, nostrils expanding for a better smell of what was approaching. The ever-present wind lifted his mane, but he held his body as still as stone.

The boy stepped closer, offering a carrot. He noticed the horse's ribs showing through its thick hide and knew that the long, stormy winter had been a hard one. While the dark horse crunched the carrots, the boy reached to pat his wooly neck, then stroked his face and mane. The two studied each other for a few minutes, then, suddenly, the dark horse was off, running toward the beach, mane and tail streaming behind him.

The boy's thoughts were still on the dark horse as he made his way home. Along the way he passed towers of rusting crab pots and piles of colorful buoys. Just beyond the stacks of fishing gear and next to a dilapidated Quonset hut stood the saddest looking creature he had ever seen.

The gray dappled mare had once been strong and beautiful, but years of neglect had broken her spirit and dulled her beauty. Day and night, through fierce winds and driving rain, she stood in the small, muddy yard. Her leg was tied with a thick line to some old tire rims, and her head hung down. Sometimes the boy would stop and speak softly to her, but she never lifted her head. He felt a pang of guilt for not saving a few carrots for her. He had been too excited about the dark horse to remember this poor animal.

The young boy had often overheard the grown-ups talk about the gray mare, whose owner was a fisherman, gone for months at a time. They said things like, "Poor old nag, barely enough food and no exercise, it's a wonder she's still alive," and "I heard the guy that owns her is gonna put her out of her misery as soon as he gets back from fishing." The boy's mother had sadly shaken her head and said, "She'd be better off if someone just cut her loose."

That night the boy slept fitfully. He dreamed of sad-faced horses caked in mud and of wild, dark horses running free in the wind. He woke before dawn, dressed quickly and quietly slipped through the front door.

As he neared the gray horse's yard, he spoke soft, comforting words to keep her calm. He opened a small pocket knife and went to work on the heavy line that held her. It was thick and stiff and took some time to saw through, but finally it fell away.

He patted the mare gently as he stepped up on the edge of a crab pot and leaned against her. She stood still as he swung his leg over her back. The boy clicked softly and nudged her with his heels. At first she did not move, then she took a few tentative steps, then a few more. Slowly, they made their way down the road.

The morning sun was turning the clouds red, as they rounded a corner and got their first glimpse of Summer Bay. The boy could feel the mare's labored breathing and his legs were damp from her perspiration, but he gently coaxed her on.

They followed the road until it became a footpath, the pounding surf below them and golden hills rising to meet steep cliffs on their right. When they came to a small stream, the boy slid from the mare's back. The gray horse drank a long time from the cold, sweet stream.

The boy reached into his parka pocket and pulled out a plump apple. He held it under the mare's nose and she took it gently with her large, yellow teeth. As she munched thoughtfully, the boy watched the juice dribble from her lips. Then he stroked her neck, said goodbye, and headed back toward town.

He looked back once, and was happy to see that she had moved up a small hill and was grazing on the tall, yellow grass. The wind picked up and blew ragged clouds across the gray afternoon sky, but the air was getting warmer and he knew that soon there would be tender new greens for her to eat. Early in the summer, the hills would be covered with hundreds of wildflowers, and later in the season there would be juicy salmonberries and tart blueberries. He smiled to himself, picturing the gray horse feasting on wild plants.

As the days went by, some people in the village thought that the old mare had finally died. But the truth was, she had never been more alive than during that lush, green summer. She regained her health and beauty and held her head high.

The boy visited Summer Bay often, and when the gray mare saw him she would always come and accept the treats he offered. Most times the dark horse would stand off by himself, and when he trotted off into the hills, the mare would follow. Sometimes the boy would spot them racing down the beach, their hooves kicking sand high in the air. When the Aleutian wind was fierce, they'd stand close together for protection. He was happy to see that the two horses had become constant companions; you could say that they were friends.

The short summer ended quickly and, all too soon, winter set in. Heavy, wet snow slid from the cliffs and blocked the road to Summer Bay. The boy would have to wait until spring to see the wild horses again.

He thought about the two horses many times that winter. When a howling storm rattled his window, the boy dreamed about his friends. He saw them standing close together for warmth, their breath a wreath of fog around their necks, sleet sliding from their hides. He pictured them pawing at snowdrifts for last year's grass and searching the beach for bits of kelp. The boy tossed and turned and prayed for spring to arrive.

When an early thaw cleared the road, the boy was the first to hike out to Summer Bay. His backpack bulged with treats for the wild horses – carrots, apples and a huge cabbage. He walked quickly, wishing his legs could go faster.

He scrambled up a hill, then turned in a slow circle, searching for the wild horses. Then he sat down to wait. He waited all morning. He waited all afternoon. His heart grew heavy as the sky darkened, and he knew he would have to leave soon. Once more his eyes searched the beach, the hills, and beyond. He began to wonder if they had survived the winter.

It was almost dark as the boy sadly stood up to leave. The wind had quieted and all was still. Just then, he heard the rustle of dry grass and saw the two horses appear from between the hills. He picked up his pack and happily rushed to greet his friends.

So now on the island of Unalaska there live two wild horses. And when the children of the village go to Summer Bay, they always bring enough apples and carrots for both. Some for the beautiful, gentle gray mare, and some for the wild, dark horse of Unalaska..

The End

Author Margarida Kondak lives in Homer, Alaska, with her husband, Doug, and daughter, Jackie. Before moving to Homer, the Kondaks lived in Unalaska, in the Aleutian Islands, for more than six years. While there, they enjoyed going to Summer Bay to hike, fish, beachcomb, and, of course, to watch the wild horses.

Mary Kondak, the illustrator, is a professional artist who now resides in Eugene, Oregon, with her husband, Dan, and daughter, Lauren. From 1982 until 1997, they lived in Unalaska, where Mary found much beauty to inspire her artwork.

Although the dark horse is no longer living, the gray horse still lives at Summer Bay with an extended family of wild horses. The children of Unalaska still love to go there and climb the golden hills to watch the growing herd. If you are ever lucky enough to visit this magical place, be sure to bring enough apples for all the wild horses.

To order more copies of this book, send $9.95 plus $2 postage ($4 for priority mail) to Wizard Works, P.O. Box 1125, Homer, AK 99603. To pay by credit card, you may e-mail your order to wizard@xyz.net, or fax it to 877-210-2665. For other books about Alaska, check out the following website: www.xyz.net/~wizard.